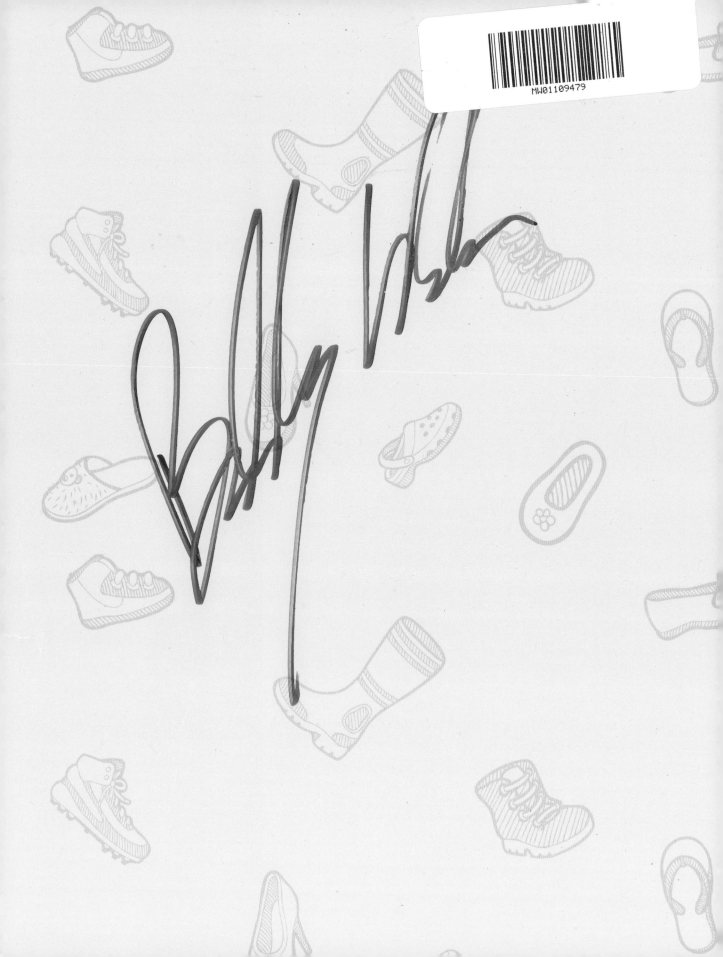

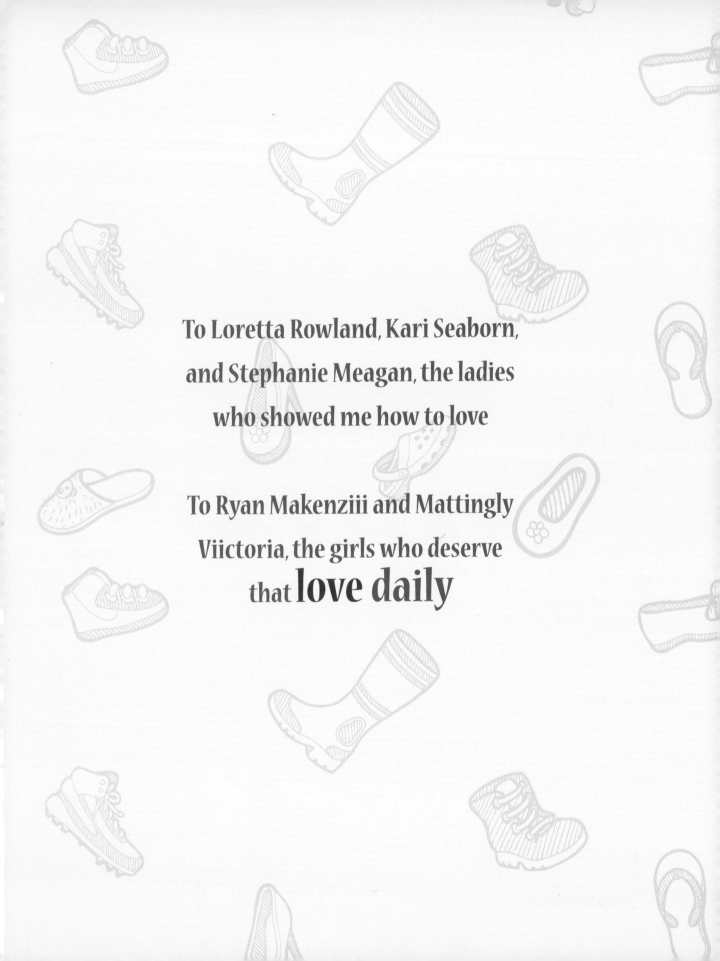

To Loretta Rowland, Kari Seaborn,
and Stephanie Meagan, the ladies
who showed me how to love

To Ryan Makenziii and Mattingly
Viictoria, the girls who deserve
that **love daily**

www.mascotbooks.com

Loretta, You Can't Wear Shoes to Bed

For more information, please contact:
Mascot Books
620 Herndon Parkway, Suite 320
Herndon, VA 20170
info@mascotbooks.com

Library of Congress Control Number: 2017960713

CPSIA Code: PR0418B
ISBN-13: 978-1-68401-330-2

Printed in the United States

Loretta,
You Can't Wear
Shoes
to Bed

written by
Bradley Weldon

Illustrated by **Mark Brayer**

Monday night, as Loretta gets ready for sleep, Mommy and Daddy help tuck her into bed.

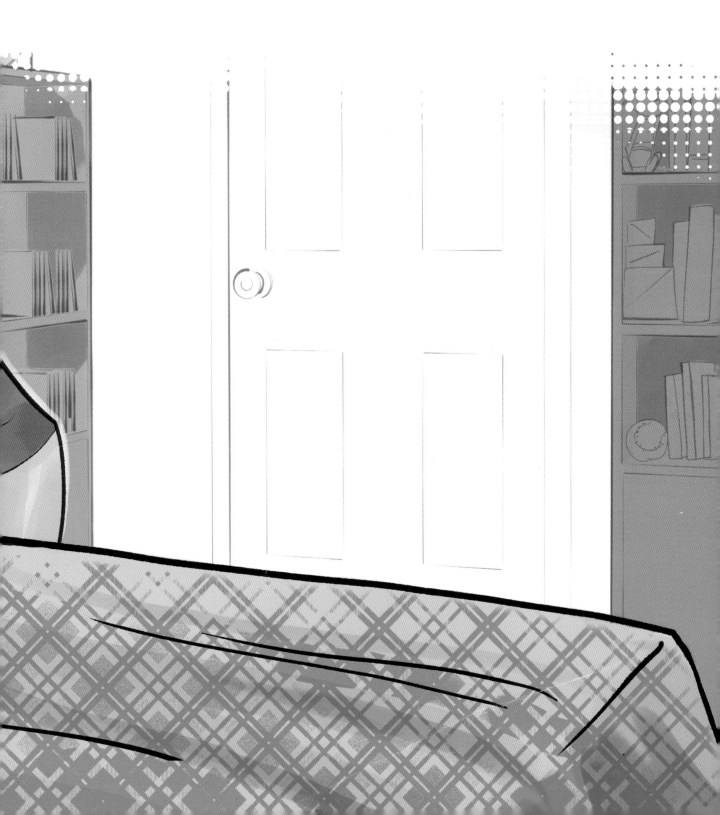

After Mommy kisses Loretta on the cheek,
Daddy kisses Loretta on the nose.

And that is when Daddy notices something
very **strange**…

Daddy looks closely at Loretta's feet and says,

"Loretta, you can't wear SHOES to bed!"

"**But Daddy,**" Loretta explains, "I need my snow boots to climb to the top of the tallest mountain in my dream tonight."

"That sounds *very adventurous*, and I'm confident you'll conquer the mountain.

But Loretta, you can't wear shoes to bed!"

Tuesday night, Mommy kisses Loretta's cheek and tucks her into bed.

Daddy looks at her feet and says, **"Loretta, you can't wear shoes to bed."**

"But Daddy, I'm attending the royal ball at the castle tonight in my dreams. I'm going to dance with the prince, and I need my fancy slippers."

"I'm sure you'll be the prettiest girl at the ball and the king and queen will approve of the new princess. **But Loretta, you can't wear shoes to bed!**"

Wednesday night, after Mommy and Daddy give kisses to Loretta, Daddy can't believe his eyes.

"Loretta, you can't wear shoes to bed!"

"But Daddy, tonight in my dreams I'm playing in the championship game. I need my cleats to score the game-winning goal!"

"I know you'll play well and score a lot of goals. You'll be the hero of the game. **But Loretta, you can't wear shoes to bed.**"

Thursday night, Mommy kisses Loretta while Daddy pulls away the blanket from Loretta's feet. Daddy is shocked at what he sees.

"Roller skates?!" Daddy asks. Now he's angry and says, **"Loretta! You CAN'T wear shoes to bed!"**

"But Daddy, how can I possibly roller skate with all my friends if I don't wear my roller skates?"

"This is the fourth night in a row that you've worn shoes to bed. I've told you that dreams can be fun and you can imagine anything you want. But for the very last time, **Loretta, you can't wear shoes to bed!**"

Friday night, before Mommy kisses Loretta's cheek and before Daddy kisses Loretta's nose, they peek under the blanket.

Mommy and Daddy are so excited that Loretta's feet and toes are bare. Daddy whispers softly, "I'm so proud that you listened and didn't wear **shoes to bed.**"

"Of course, I don't have **shoes** on for tonight's dream! Everyone knows...Daddy, you can't wear **shoes** in the ocean."

About the Author

Bradley "Ducky" Weldon might be new to the dream-writing profession, but he's been living in a dream world for many years. He has worked as a baseball umpire, doughnut flipper, Wild West train robber, cable TV auction host, professional seat filler at the Radio Music Awards, and substitute teacher. For the last few years, he's been a private process server. But of the many jobs he has had (and lost), he's most proud of being a daddy to his two daughters, Ryan Makenziii and Mattingly Viictoria.

Community Outreach

Want Bradley Weldon to visit your school or daycare? He will donate his time and travel anywhere in the country to personally read and distribute sponsored copies of *Loretta, You Can't Wear Shoes to Bed*.

After reading to the group, he will conduct an activity in which students can wear autographed shoes and discuss their own desired dreams, just like Loretta in the book. After the activity, students will receive their own copy of the book and create personal thank-you letters to be delivered to their classroom sponsor. To be a classroom sponsor or purchase individual copies to donate, please contact:

Bradley Weldon
405-885-2422
bradleyweldon@yahoo.com
www.bradleyweldon.com

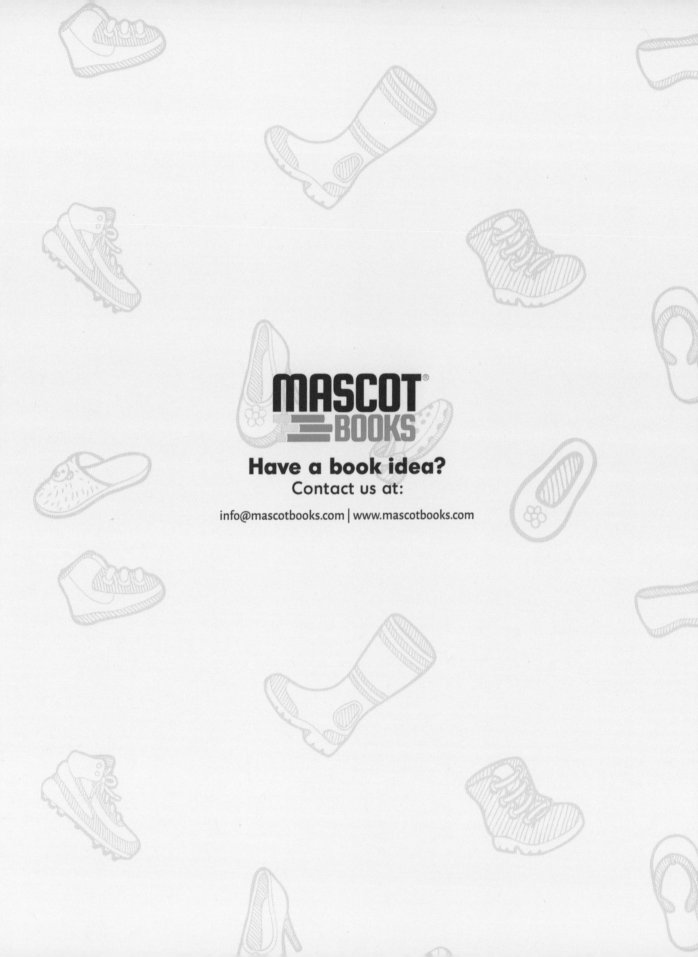